1 3 AUG 2007

3 0 OCT 2007

0 5 DEC 2007

0 3 MAR 2009

2 6 MAY 2009

2 3 JUN 2009

2 4 AUG 2009

1 9 AUG 2009

2 0 NOV 2010

1 1 JUL 2011

1 0 SEP 2012

1 5 OCT 2012

GRINDLEY, Sally

- 9 APR 2013

Mouldylocks and
the three Clares

- 5 JAN 2013

# Mouldylocks
## and the
# Three Clares

Written by **Sally Grindley**
Illustrated by Nathan Reed

A & C Black • London

First published 2007 by
A & C Black Publishers Ltd
38 Soho Square, London, W1D 3HB

www.acblack.com

Text copyright © 2007 Sally Grindley
Illustrations copyright © 2007 Nathan Reed

ISBN 0-7136-7753-8
ISBN 978-0-7136-7753-9

A CIP catalogue for this book is available from the British Library.

This book is produced using paper that is made from wood grown in
managed, sustainable forests. It is natural, renewable and recyclable.
The logging and manufacturing processes conform to the
environmental regulations of the country of origin.

Printed and bound in Singapore by Tien Wah Press (Pte) Ltd

# Chapter One

High up in the clouds, at the top of a tangled beanstalk, there was an enormous castle. It was owned by a very ugly giant called Mouldylocks, who lived all alone – apart from his big, fat hen, which laid piles of golden eggs.

One evening, Mouldylocks was sitting in front of the fire polishing his gold coins, when he said to the hen, "A giant needs a wife. I am going to find myself a wife."

"Cluck, brrrrrup," said the hen, as she laid another egg.

The next morning, Mouldylocks brushed his hair (for the first time in years), and slid down the beanstalk. When he reached the bottom, he set off along the road towards the nearby village.

As soon as they saw him coming, the villagers were terrified. They ran into their houses and bolted their doors.

The giant rapped on one door after
another. Nobody answered.
"Come out!" he roared. "I'm only looking
for someone to be my wife."

But everyone stayed hidden inside,
quaking in their boots.

"Be like that," growled the giant. "You don't know what you're missing."
Then he stomped off.

# Chapter Two

It wasn't long before Mouldylocks
came to an old bridge, which led to
some woods.

Ahead of him, along a narrow path,
he could see three cottages.

The first cottage was big, the second was tiny, and the third was medium-sized. At the beginning of the path was a sign which read 'Here live the 3 Clares'.

"Aha!" said Mouldylocks. "Three Clares! Perhaps one of them will be my wife."

He went up to the big cottage. Sunflowers and hollyhocks were growing in the garden, there was a pile of logs by the door, and rock music was blaring from the open windows.

"Excellent," said the giant to himself. "A woman who grows big flowers, chops logs and likes rock music will suit me well." He knocked loudly on the door.

After a few moments, a large woman with a big, pink nose poked her head out of a window. "Who's that knocking so loudly on my door?" she said.

"I am Mouldylocks," said the giant.
"You can say that again," said the woman.
"I am Mouldylocks," repeated the giant.
"I live in an enormous castle and have
riches beyond your wildest dreams.
I am looking for a wife."

"A wife, eh?" said the woman. "I am Great Big Clare. An enormous castle and riches beyond my wildest dreams sound good to me."

"Then come back with me now," said Mouldylocks, thinking how lucky he was to have found such an ample woman.

Great Big Clare wasn't sure how lucky she was to have found such a mouldy giant, but she didn't need to be asked twice. She ran down the stairs, grabbed hold of the giant's hand, then they marched back along the road and up the beanstalk together.

# Chapter Three

Great Big Clare couldn't believe her eyes when she entered the giant's castle. "There's more gold on the lid of your teapot than in the whole of my cottage," she said, and she was happy to think that soon it would all belong to her.

Within minutes, she had moved her clothes into the giant's wardrobe and made herself at home.

Mouldylocks wasn't happy with Great Big Clare. He quickly discovered that:

1. She was bossy.

2. She snored.

3. The porridge she made had lumps in it.

4. She stood in front of the mirror plucking hairs from her chin.

5. She refused to chop the logs.

The final straw was when she turfed him out of his comfy chair, sat in it herself, and forced him to sit on a stool.

Mouldylocks seethed all night long, then the next morning he said, "Great Big Clare, I do not want you for my wife. You must go down the beanstalk and never come back again."

Great Big Clare cried and shouted and stamped her feet, but Mouldylocks would not change his mind, so she climbed down the beanstalk and stomped all the way back to her cottage.

# Chapter Four

A few weeks later, Mouldylocks was playing tiddlywinks with his gold coins, when he said to his hen, "I'm going to try again to find a wife."

"Cluck, brrrrrup," said the hen, as she laid another egg.

The giant put on his very best clothes,
polished his boots (for the first time
ever), slid down the beanstalk, and set
off along the road
to the village.

Once again, the villagers ran inside their
houses, bolting their doors behind them.
Mouldylocks didn't care. He kept on
going until he reached the path at the
edge of the woods.

He walked straight past Great Big Clare's cottage and on to the next. The tiny little cottage had a tiny little garden full of tiny little flowers. Piccolo music drifted out through the open windows and there was a delicious smell of cakes.

"Mmmm," said the giant to himself.

"It's a long time since anyone baked
me a cake."
He bent down and rapped on the front
door. After a few moments, it was opened
by a tiny little woman.
"Mind you don't knock my door down,"
she said, but she smiled at him sweetly.

"I am Mouldylocks," said the giant.
"I live in an enormous castle and have riches beyond your wildest dreams. I am looking for a wife."
"I am Tiny Wee Clare," said the woman. "I have heard all about you from my sister. She is a fool if she could not make you happy. I will be a better wife."

Mouldylocks was delighted, even if she was a bit small, so he picked her up and carried her back to his castle.

# Chapter Five

Tiny Wee Clare couldn't believe her eyes when she saw such wealth. "There is more gold on the handle of your toilet than in the whole of my tiny litttle cottage," she said, and she was happy to think that one day it would all belong to her.

She quickly set about making herself at home, covering his shelves with tiny little nick-nacks.

Mouldylocks wasn't happy with Tiny Wee Clare. He soon discovered that:

1. She was only big enough to chop twigs.

2. She grew daisies in his egg cups.

3. The cakes she baked were the size of sugar lumps.

4. She was too small to make the bed.

5. He kept
losing her.

When she nearly drowned running his
bath, Mouldylocks had had enough.

"Tiny Wee Clare," he said the next
morning, "I do not want you for my wife.
You must go down the beanstalk and
never come back again."

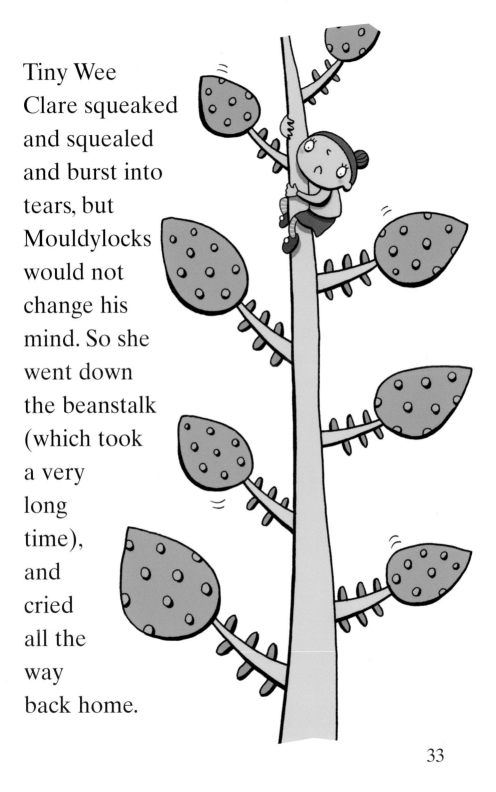

Tiny Wee Clare squeaked and squealed and burst into tears, but Mouldylocks would not change his mind. So she went down the beanstalk (which took a very long time), and cried all the way back home.

# Chapter Six

A few weeks later, Mouldylocks was playing carpet bowls with his gold coins when he said to his hen, "I am going to have one last try at finding a wife."

"Cluck, brrrrrup," said the hen, as she laid another egg.

The giant put on his very, very best clothes, shaved himself (which was possibly a mistake), slid down the beanstalk and set off along the road.

He stomped straight through the village, across the old bridge, into the woods and past the first two cottages.

When he reached the medium-sized
cottage, he was pleased to see smoke
billowing from the chimney. The garden
was mostly decking, with a few bushes
dotted about. A rich smell of roasting
meat came through the windows.
"Who needs cakes if there's a roast
on offer?" he grinned.

Mouldylocks knocked on the door.
After a few moments it was
opened by a not-too-tall,
not-too-short, not-too-fat,
not-too-thin woman.
"Can I help you?"
she asked.

Mouldylocks stared at her and was pleased with what he saw.

"I am Mouldylocks," he said. "I live in an enormous castle and have riches beyond your wildest dreams. I am looking for a wife."

"I am Medium-sized Clare," said the woman. "I have heard all about you from my sisters, but I like to make up my own mind about things. I will come with you and see how we get on."

Mouldylocks was delighted. Apart from anything else, Medium-sized Clare was much better looking than her sisters. He took her gently by the hand and led her back to his castle.

# Chapter Seven

Medium-sized Clare couldn't believe her eyes when she saw the giant's gold. "You have all the riches in the world," she said. "What can I do to make you happy?"

Mouldylocks gave her a very long list.
"I will do all those things for you with
pleasure," said Medium-sized Clare.
She paused, as though waiting for the
giant to say something in return.
"Good," was all he
said. "That's what
I like to hear."

Over the next few weeks, Medium-sized
Clare chopped wood and cooked and
cleaned and laid fires and trimmed the
beanstalk.

She didn't snore and she didn't pluck hairs
from her chin; she didn't grow things in his
tea cups and she didn't
keep getting lost.

She made the best porridge Mouldylocks
had ever tasted in his life, and she made
the bed so well that he slept like a tree
trunk.

Mouldylocks was so happy that one morning he said to his hen, "Medium-sized Clare is the perfect wife for me. I am going to marry her."

"Cluck, brrrrup," said the hen, as she laid another egg.

Mouldylocks found Medium-sized Clare standing at the top of the beanstalk, gazing down to the ground below. "Medium-sized Clare," he said, "you know how to make me happy. I will have you as my wife."

Medium-sized Clare looked at him in astonishment. "Giant Mouldylocks," she said, "I wouldn't be your wife if you gave me all the gold in the world. Not once have you asked me what you can do to make me happy. Not once have you lifted a finger to help me. Not once have you said thank you. I would rather be poor for the rest of my days than stay here with you."

With that, she slid down the beanstalk.

Mouldylocks bellowed and bawled and thundered around, but Medium-sized Clare didn't even look back.

After one last howl of anger, the giant stomped back into his castle, sat down in front of his gold and began to count it. "Bah!" he growled. "Who needs a wife anyway?"

"Cluck, brrrrup," said the hen, and she laid another egg.